whenever there is ... send for ...

# Kung-Fu
## Pigs

Scholastic Children's Books,
Commonwealth House, 1–19 New Oxford Street,
London, WC1A 1NU, UK
A division of Scholastic Ltd
London ~ New York ~ Toronto ~ Sydney ~ Auckland
Mexico City ~ New Delhi ~ Hong Kong

First published in the UK by Scholastic Ltd, 2003

ISBN 0 439 97722 3

Printed and bound by Nørhaven Paperback A/S, Denmark

10 9 8 7 6 5 4 3 2 1

# Kung-Fu pigs

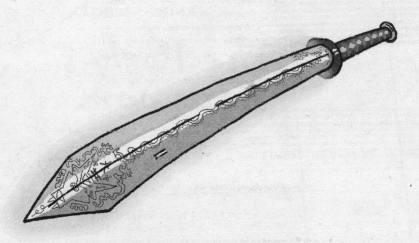

## The Magic Sword of Gung-Ho

## Keith Brumpton

SCHOLASTIC

THE LO-FAT HILLS

THE CAVE
WITH
NO NAME
Home of the

CHIN CHIN
(Rinki's home)

PORKAIDO

KNOCKNEEDO

# The Pork-i Kingdom

BRIDGE OF THE
SEVENTH GOLDFISH

NO-PEKIN
Capital city, home to
our great and noble emperor

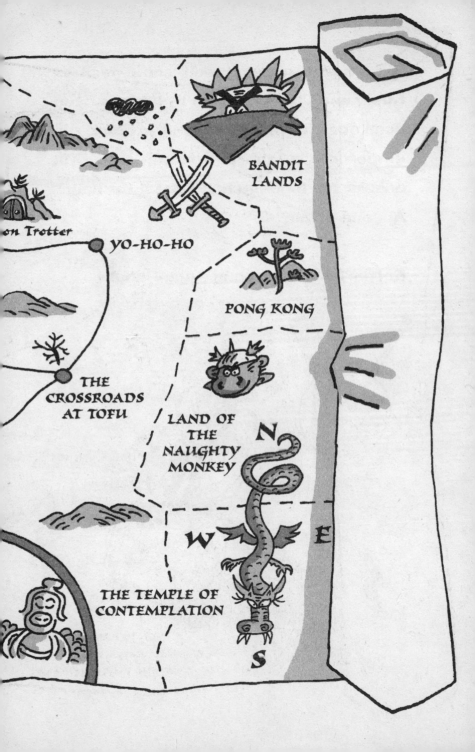

Once again, pig and wolf come face to face and things aren't looking too good for the pigs. Who will protect the emperor? Is there anyone who will answer his high-pitched squeal for help? Anyone at all?

Better bang that gong, Ping-Pong!

# The Magic Sword of Gung-Ho

**Translated from the original Pork-i manuscript by** Keith Brumpton

## PROLOGUE

I am Oinky No Ho, adviser to the Great Emperor Ping-Pong, and priest of the Monastery of Wu-dah-ling. I am here to tell you of the Kung-Fu Pigs, and of how they fought to defend our lands against that most evil traitor, the Crimson Trotter (he who keeps the company of wolves). In this tale you will learn of bandits and of foul play. Of magic swords and evil spells. And so, honourable stranger, let us begin...

# CHAPTER 1

*"Beware the wolf at the door. Especially if he's carrying a big stick."*
General Minimota, 12th century

Deep, deep in the caves below the Lo-Fat Hills, something stirred. No, not a spoon. Something more evil than a spoon.

There was a spot in these caves (if you walked far enough), where they opened out to form something like a small room.

This was the same spot where the flames were now leaping high against stone walls, casting giant, flickering shadows. And standing there, all robed in red, stood the Crimson Trotter; the most wanted pig in the land, sworn enemy of the emperor, Master of the Dark Arts, sometime painter of watercolours.

He gave an evil laugh as he went about his nefarious business. He was busy casting a spell. A spell that would create a magic sword.

"One sword to rule over all the lands of Pong. One sword with magic powers beyond the dreams of pigs! One sword with attractive jewels in the handle!"

So saying, he thrust the sword into the flames and began to honk a strange incantation:

Sword be strong, now forged in flame. Fight until you break And deadly be your aim!

"Ahem!"

From out of the shadows a figure suddenly approached. A wolf, tall in stature, with dark staring eyes. His name was Gung-Ho, and he was a rebel general. But even generals lived in fear of the Crimson Trotter. Gung-Ho lowered his eyes and made a deep bow. The Crimson Trotter remained silhouetted against the flames, but waved Gung-Ho forward. Then, into the general's furry, battle-scarred paws, he thrust the magic sword which he had just forged.

"Take this sword, Gung-Ho, and await my orders. This sword will win us the kingdom of Ping-Pong and all his riches."

As he finished these words, the Crimson Trotter burst into laughter and that same laughter echoed all the way along the dark, damp caves, until it was as if a thousand evil pigs laughed there, instead of just one...

# CHAPTER 2

*"To listen is sometimes harder than to speak, but it is only by listening that we learn in which direction we must travel."*
Princess Shimsham, 3rd century

In the garden of the wise old philosopher, Oinky No Ho, there was a large gong. It was the size of two pigs laid end to end, and was only to be sounded in times of great danger.

So when the young noble-pig, Rinki, heard the sound of a gong drifting out across the paddy fields and orchards of his home village, he knew what he must do. Rinki was one of the three Kung-Fu Pigs for whom the gong tolled. On hearing that sound, his orders were to hurry at once to the emperor's palace and await orders.

Rinki threw down his trowel, apologized to the pig whose foot it had landed on, and then hurried off to find a swift horse...

In the hometown of Stinki the samurai pig, the same gong had also sounded. Stinki knew his orders well, like any good samurai. He hurriedly finished the bowl of rice he was scoffing and began to strap on his armour...

And what of the third of the Kung-Fu Pigs, the fair Dinki, pig-tailed priestess and great beauty? She had heard the gong too, and hurried from her temple, wondering why she had been summoned and what adventures might lie ahead…

Later that day, as evening fell, the three Kung-Fu Pigs arrived at the gates of a magnificent garden. It was the garden of Oinky No Ho, who was there to greet them.

The three Kung-Fu Pigs bowed low before their master and waited for him to speak.

"Honourable Rinki, most excellent Stinki, learned Dinki … thank you all for answering the summons of the gong and coming so quickly."

"It was our honour to obey," answered Stinki. "But ... I ... er ... don't suppose you have any supper left?" Stinki's thoughts were never far from food.

Oinky No Ho showed them through into the garden and there they were given bowls of water to wash their dusty trotters, and cups of warm green tea.

"What's the problem?" asked Rinki, ever impatient.

"When will we get to fight?" added Stinki, who quite enjoyed a bit of unarmed conflict now and then.

Only Dinki remained silent, waiting for their guru to speak.

Finally the old pig rose slowly to his feet, (which was the only speed he could rise these days). His snout wore a serious expression.

"It is none of these. I have summoned you here to face a threat more terrible still."

"More terrible than dragons?! Impossible!" snorted Rinki.

Oinky No Ho continued, sternly. "There is evil magic at work in our land. A rebel general called Gung-Ho has formed an army and has attacked the emperor's northern parts. He is the fiercest of wolves and the emperor's armies flee before him."

"A wolf!" laughed Stinki. "We can easily handle wolves!"

Oinky No Ho began pacing the lawn slowly (he did everything slowly, for was he not the oldest pig in the empire?)

"It is not Gung-Ho who is the problem. It is the fact that he uses magic."

"What kind of magic?" asked Dinki.

"He has a magic sword. A sword they say no one can ever hope to defeat. The sort of sword perhaps only the Crimson Trotter could have made."

made by the *Crimson Trotter*

Rinki's expression changed. "Did these rebels not attack a market just a few days ago?"

Oinky No Ho nodded his wise old head. "Yes ... and terrible was the result to behold…"

# CHAPTER 3

Jugglers and acrobats entertained the crowds. Deals were being struck and pockets fleeced, until SUDDENLY…

A bunch of traders took up their bamboo staffs and tried to put up a fight...

But they were no match for the rebel forces.

At the word of command, it flew up into the air and began carving a swathe through the market place.

Pigs tumbled out of its path, ripe melons were sliced in two, market stalls splintered like matchwood. Everything had to give way to the Magic Sword of Gung-Ho!

# CHAPTER 4

*"Is the moon no longer there just because we can not see it for the clouds?"* Oki-Koki, 2nd Dynasty

Dinki shook her head when she heard the story of Gung-Ho's raid on the market.

"No pig can sleep safely in his sty while that evil warlord is still free!"

Oinky No Ho nodded wisely, which was the only type of nod he had. "And not just that, Dinki. I fear that Gung-Ho plans to take over the whole of the emperor's kingdom!"

This was too much for Stinki, whose loyalty to the emperor knew no bounds. He leapt to his trotters and grabbed his helmet and bow.

Oinky No Ho laid a trotter on the samurai's broad shoulders. "More haste, less speed, brave Stinki. First we need to find a way for you to take on this magic and win."

Rinki turned to the old guru. "You are wise and powerful, Oinky No Ho. Can you not give us magic of our own? Magic that would help defeat the rebels?"

Stinki nodded enthusiastically. "Yes ... magic! That's just what we need!"

"Just what you DON'T need," interrupted Dinki. "Don't you boys know how dangerous magic can be in the wrong hands?"

the wrong hands

Outside, a gust of wind rattled the shutters of the old house. A storm was brewing. The wise and venerable guru gazed out at the darkening sky and pondered.

"Magic? Perhaps... But then again, perhaps not..."

He wandered out of the room without another word, and the Kung-Fu Pigs were left not knowing what would happen next. In the distance, thunder began to rumble...

# CHAPTER 5

*"One day the apple is perfect and ripe, but if not plucked then, it turns sour for life..."*

YoYo-Yang, poet, 2nd Dynasty

While the Kung-Fu Pigs readied for the struggle ahead, Gung-Ho's rebel army was sweeping all before it. No, not with brooms, you fools ... with the Magic Sword! Pigs of high society fled in the night. Peasants and their families did a runner. Even the emperor's best troops scattered like confetti on a windy day.

As we join them, Gung-Ho's troops have just captured the town of Knockneedo. The rebel leader himself leads the procession down the main street, his wolfish grin greeting all those who dare look in his direction. And in his scabbard, he wears the Magic Sword, its terrible power ready to be unleashed at a moment's notice...

Gung-Ho dismounted from his horse, gave orders to secure the town for the night, and then slipped away from the rest of his men. He hurried down a set of old steps, following a map which had been thrust into his paws by a messenger earlier that day. The steps led to a set of underground passageways running beneath the city. Dark, gloomy passageways, built by pigs, so barely tall enough for a wolf like Gung-Ho to pass through. He turned a corner, bent almost in two, when suddenly a torch flared in his evil, wolfish eyes.

"Halt!"

Gung-Ho jumped nervously. He heard familiar laughter.

"Frightened of the dark, Gung-Ho?"

From out of the darkness stepped a squat figure, dressed from head to toe in a red silk robe.

Gung-Ho bowed down low. When he spoke, there was a slight tremor in his voice.

Most excellent master...

"Yes, that's me," nodded the crimson one.

"The plan goes well. We have captured many towns and tomorrow we ride on the emperor's palace itself!"

"What news of the Kung-Fu Pigs?"

There was a pause. A raindrop splashed into a dank puddle.

"None as yet," Gung-Ho answered. "But my spies are watching everywhere."

The Crimson Trotter nodded his head slowly. "It must be so. Defeat them and the whole kingdom will be ours!"

"With my Magic Sword — our Magic Sword…" hissed Gung-Ho,

"Yes, yes, I get the picture, Gung-Ho. Take your leave now, and continue our work."

The wolf warrior bowed obediently. His steps echoed off into the distance, and the Crimson Trotter stood for a moment, revelling in the thought of the Kung-Fu Pigs and how futile their attempts would be to resist his magic.

# CHAPTER 6

*"Better the plain clogs of a peasant, than the fine shoe of a nobleman that doesn't fit."*
Wei-Hei-Hei, poet, 2nd century

Stinki had polished his helmet for the twenty-third time when finally the great cherry-wood door swung open and there before them stood Oinky No Ho.

"What magic will he give us?" wondered Rinki to himself. "Will it be an arrow that never misses, or a cloak to conjure up storms?"

Oinky No Ho smiled to himself. He was holding a simple pair of silk slippers.

"Are those magic slippers?" asked Stinki, excitedly.

The wise old pig nodded.

"Will they make us run fast as lightning?"

Oinky No Ho shook his head. "No, my impatient student, these magic shoes will give you but one power..."

The Kung-Fu Pigs leant forward as one,
even Dinki was curious now...
"...The power of ... invisibility."

Rinki jumped with excitement. "Amazing!"

"Splendid news!"
shouted Stinki,
thumping the table
with his trotter.
"No one will
stand a
chance
against us now!"

Only Dinki had yet to speak. She had just one question for their wise old master. "You have just one pair?"

Oinky No Ho nodded. "One pair is all you will need."

Rinki and Stinki looked a little cross.

"So who will wear them?" asked Rinki.

"Me, of course," honked Stinki. "I'm the warrior here."

"In your dreams!" retorted Rinki.

Oinky No Ho raised his arms to stop the bickering. "Whosoever's trotters fit the slippers shall wear them."

Rinki was the first to try on the Slippers of Invisibility, but struggle as he might, his noble trotters were just too big.

Stinki tried next, already sure that he was the one. "Yes... I think ... just give me a mo..."

But the samurai would have needed more than a moment to squeeze his giant trotters into those delicate little slippers.

Frustrated, he gave up and flung the
footwear across the room. The slippers
landed right at
Dinki's feet.

"It's ridiculous!" Stinki complained,
sulkily. "Fancy giving the magic to a ... to
a girl!"

Yes, as you may by now have guessed, and as Oinky No Ho probably knew all along, the Magic Slippers of Invisibility fitted Dinki. Like a glove (except that unlike gloves she wore them on her feet).

"It's not fair!" spluttered Rinki, equally unhappy at this turn of events. It was a while before he realized that Dinki wasn't around to hear his protests. Or if she was, he couldn't see her any more. She had vanished!

"Honourable Dinki?" whispered our young hero, sorry for his quick temper.

"Yes," she replied, from somewhere over by the shutters.

"Amazing! You've completely vanished."

"Very strange!" added Stinki, still a little jealous.

Oinky No Ho allowed himself the luxury of a smile. "So, noble pigs, you see how well this magic can work?"

Rinki and Stinki bowed before their elderly guru.

"Couldn't you make just one more pair?" pleaded Stinki. "Where would be the harm in that?"

"You will have to trust your poor, humble adviser," replied Oinky No Ho. "One pair will be sufficient. Now take the magic I have given you and seek out Gung-Ho before it is too late."

The door to the room had opened ahead of them, and they could hear the still-invisible Dinki's voice echo across the room towards them:

Come on, you two, the master is right, there's work to be done!

Realizing that Oinky No Ho was not about to change his mind, Rinki and Stinki gathered up their weapons and hurried after their invisible friend.

"Good luck, Kung-Fu Pigs," their master called out after them. "Be wise and use your magic well!"

# CHAPTER 7

*"The wisest emperor does not think himself wise at all."*
Gang-Wei, philoso-pig, 3rd Dynasty

That most noble and wise emperor, Ping-Pong, was in a terrible tizzy. He felt like bursting into tears. And it wasn't for fear that his kingdom might be lost or his armies defeated.

No, it was because the royal cook had just told him that owing to a shortage of food supplies there would only be enough for eight courses of lunch instead of the usual ten.

"I cannot believe it! How cruel and thoughtless a world we live in!"

He blew on the sleeve of his fine silk robe and began sobbing big snuffly sobs. A courtier ran up to dab his tears.

"Why is everything so upside down today?" he asked the courtier, whose name I am afraid, escapes me.

"All is confusion, oh noble and wise emperor, because the evil rebel Gung-Ho has captured yet another city and is advancing through your lands like a raging river through defenceless fields."

Ping-Pong began to sob even more.

"And that means I can't have a proper lunch?"

"He has cut off your supplies, Excellency."

The young emperor rallied himself a little. "Why did no one tell me of this? Did Oinky  No Ho not send for the Kung-Fu Pigs? I believe I saw them arrive earlier this morning. They at least will save me from this Gung-Ho, will they not?"

But when he looked up, the courtier had vanished. Everywhere in the palace was the sight of pigs fleeing. Panic is like swine fever – it travels very quickly.

The emperor watched in sadness as all around him his servants and courtiers rushed out into the streets, taking with them everything they could carry.

Poor Ping-Pong, abandoned in his own palace. He could hardly bring himself to finish his eight-course lunch, though of course he tried his best.

What a foolish young pig the emperor was, to think of his stomach when he could have been saving his bacon!

# CHAPTER 8

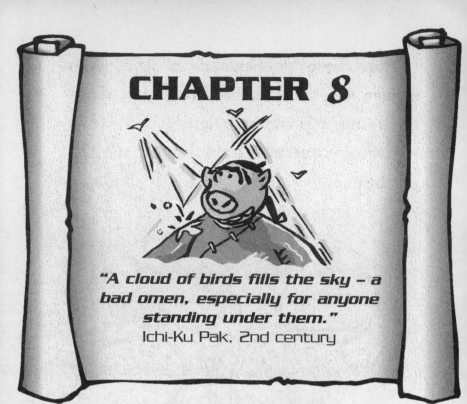

*"A cloud of birds fills the sky – a bad omen, especially for anyone standing under them."*
Ichi-Ku Pak, 2nd century

Just a hundred miles from the palace, by the Bridge of the Seventh Goldfish, the Emperor's Guard prepared to make their final stand.

They were determined to fight, even though they had all heard rumours of the Lord Gung-Ho and his Magic Sword. As the sun rose, it sparkled on their armour and gave a brave-looking gleam to all those rows of little piggy eyes.

"We must fight to save our emperor," their general told them, not sounding too convinced himself.

Suddenly there was a cloud of dust in the distance and the sound of drums.

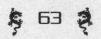

No, it wasn't a heavy metal band, it was the evil Gung-Ho and his advancing army. The Emperor's Guard gripped their spears tightly, ready for action.

THUD THUD

THUD

The general honked out his last minute instructions: "Stand in line, lads, remember your orders... A gold coin for every pig who dies bravely..."

Suddenly into view rode a single warrior, galloping forward on his grey stallion. It was Gung-Ho, and great clouds of dust were thrown up by the hooves of his mount. He was galloping straight towards the massed ranks of the emperor's troops. Surely he didn't mean to attack them alone?

The soldiers looked at each other and began to smile. They had never encountered such a foolish wolf before. Did he really think he could defeat them all, single-pawed? They raised their spears, ready for action, expecting an easy victory, when...

Gung-Ho dismounted and drew his sword! The Magic Sword given to him by the Crimson Trotter! The mere sight of this mighty weapon seemed to hypnotize the emperor's army, for none of them moved a muscle.

Then that most evil of wolves, the Lord Gung-Ho, muttered the spell he had been taught:

Sword of steel forged by the forces of night. Now do your worst and put these pigs to flight!

At once the sword left his paw and began to fly through the air of its own accord. The mere sight of this was enough for many of the emperor's loyal troops, who turned curly-tail and fled. Those who stayed watched open-mouthed in terror as Gung-Ho's sword wheeled towards them. It fought anyone who dared resist. And who could resist a sword flashing so fast, and spinning so swiftly, and presenting no target against which to fight back?

Gung-Ho watched as the emperor's army fled the bridge. And he smiled to himself contentedly. The emperor's palace now lay before him, undefended. The Crimson Trotter would surely be pleased with the way things had gone!

But what, might you wonder, had become of that great and noble emperor, Ping-Pong? He was hard at work. Hard at work trying to cram all his treasures and belongings into a large trunk. He found himself alone in the great palace, and though he had vowed to stay and fight to the last, now that he *was* the last, this suddenly didn't seem such a good idea.

"Where are my Kung-Fu Pigs?" he sobbed to himself. "Where are the Kung-Fu Pigs who are supposed to save me?"

# CHAPTER 9

*"Always journey with hope. It is the most pleasant of companions."*
Yi-Ha, Bong Dynasty

The roads circling the palace were much busier than usual. As far as the eye could see (or both eyes, if you have the full set), pigs were running, hurrying, scrambling to save their possessions before the arrival of Gung-Ho and his bandit army.

Stinki the samurai was angered to see such disloyalty to the emperor.

"Stay and fight with us!" he called out.
The only one to stop was
an old peasant pig.

"Have you not heard, Samurai? The Lord Gung-Ho has defeated the emperor's army at the Bridge of the Seventh Goldfish. That twerp of an emperor is done for. They say even the Kung-Fu Pigs have fled!" And with that, he hurried off, tottering from side to side because he was carrying a large sack of rice on his head.

Dinki had to stop Stinki from running after the old pig. "Leave him! It is our fight now. No one else will take on Gung-Ho and his magic."

Rinki nodded. "She's right. Let's head for the crossroads at Tofu, we can cut off the rebels there!"

"Agreed."

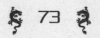

So the Kung-Fu Pigs hurried from the city and out into the countryside where a distant thunderstorm continued to rumble like the insides of a hungry wolf...

The crossroads at Tofu consisted of three dusty paths that met beneath the trunk of a withered old tree.

It was noon when the Kung-Fu Pigs arrived there, exhausted after their long journey. They only had one pony between them, which Rinki and Stinki had shared, saying that Dinki couldn't expect to ride on the pony AND have the magic slippers as well.

Stinki leapt down from the saddle and at once inspected the ground.

"Hoofprints. And these hooves weren't shod by any local blacksmith ... look!"

Rinki examined the hoofprints. "You're right. Square hooves. They only use those in Tchu-Tchin-Tchu Province!"

"Home of the evil Gung-Ho," said Stinki. "So ... he can't be very far away..."

As if on cue, two wolves in silk tunics
appeared from behind the wizened old tree
and made a grab for Rinki. But he was too
quick for them and in a flash he had leapt
to safety, whilst Stinki, ever
alert, had whipped out
his fighting staff.

Hah Soh!

Ha Hah!

So Hah!

Rinki and Stinki battled to overcome the
first two wolves, but then two more
sprang out, and then two
more…

…and then two more,
until…

…our two heroes
were completely
surrounded.

"Looks like quite a fight!" laughed Stinki, still not too worried.

"Backs to the wall, isn't that how we like it?" agreed Rinki.

And the battle continued, with the two Kung-Fu Pigs pitted against the fearsome wolves of Gung-Ho's rebel army.

While Rinki and Stinki were fighting for all their worth, Dinki found herself pursued by a group of rebels on horseback, and it was all she could do to stay ahead of them. She could hear the swish of their swords as they drew closer and closer. The wolf warriors laughed, convinced that the fight was as good as won, when suddenly, to their amazement, the young priestess vanished. Into thin air! Dinki had slipped on Oinky No Ho's magic slippers just in the nick of time... The rebels searched in vain wondering what trickery was afoot.

Meanwhile, Rinki and Stinki were fighting hard, but they were slowly being driven back by weight of numbers.

"Where's that priestess?" yelled the samurai, whilst flying acrobatically through the air. "I thought she was supposed to be helping us!"

Some help!

"Give her a chance!" Rinki shouted back, tumbling down from the tree. "She won't let us down."

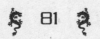

Their conversation was interrupted by the arrival of Gung-Ho himself, dressed in ceremonial armour. He towered over the rest of his followers.

Seeing the foolish pigs putting up more of a fight then he had expected, Gung-Ho didn't hang around. He drew his magic sword. The battlefield seemed to fall silent. It was eerie. The mystical power of the Crimson Trotter's sword was terrible to behold.

# CHAPTER 10

*"The outcome of the battle is never known until the fat pig sings."*
General Minimoto's *Art of Warfare*

Rinki, master of the Kung-Fu arts, and Stinki, so deadly with his bow ... there were few armies who could hold out against these two heroes. And how they leapt and spun, and ducked and weaved. What moves they conjured up.

But perhaps this would be a different battle to those they usually fought. Rinki looked up to see the Magic Sword of Gung-Ho spinning towards his friend, the samurai.

Luckily Stinki's armour saved him from injury, but even so fine a warrior as that brave pig couldn't hold off the magic blade for long.

"Help!" he honked.

Rinki tried to come to his companion's assistance, but his path was blocked by the sword. And that bewitched blade was too much even for the noble Rinki.

He was forced back towards the watching, grinning figure of Gung-Ho. And then into the arms of his henchmen.

The rebel wolf's cruel eyes flashed with evil delight as the two Kung-Fu Pigs were led away, captive. He placed the Magic Sword back into its scabbard.

But in his gloating he had completely ignored the fact that there were three little pigs to contend with. Perhaps he thought the priestess Dinki too small to be a threat to his new-found might? A slip of a girl … what could she do?

Dinki, out of sight and out of mind, watched as Gung-Ho rallied his troops, ready to enter the emperor's palace.

As a priestess of the Oinko Order, Dinki had no love of fighting. The wise word was her weapon of choice, but she knew that against Gung-Ho, even a very strong word would not be enough.

Oinky No Ho had given her the Slippers of Invisibility and now was the time to act… Gung-Ho's sword was still nestling in its scabbard, in a belt hung around his waist. Dinki watched nervously as the rebel leader strode towards his grey stallion. Once he was upon his horse there would be no catching him – even with the help of Oinky No Ho's magic.

Young Dinki seized her chance and made a grab for the magic blade. If this went wrong it was the end of her, the end of the Kung-Fu Pigs, and the end of the emperor and his kingdom!

The sword slid easily from its scabbard and into her trotters. Gung-Ho couldn't believe his eyes. The magic weapon was out of the scabbard before he knew what was happening. And then out of reach altogether.

Dinki felt the power of its magic at once. More powerful even than the magic of Oinky No Ho. A different magic ... darker ... harder to control. She could feel the presence of the sword's maker, the Crimson Trotter, looking down on her. He tried to communicate but she blotted his words from her mind.

"Kung-Fu is not fought just with the trotters but also with the mind..." so sayeth the guru Oinky No Ho.

Dinki tried to focus on the sword itself. "Sword! Rescue my friends!" she whispered, once she was certain it was within her control. On cue the sword flew up into the air. But would it follow her commands, or return to its previous master?

To Dinki's relief the sword sped towards those soldiers of Gung-Ho's who were guarding Rinki and Stinki. Gung-Ho was still in a state of shock. "What's happening?" he mumbled.

In a flash, Rinki and Stinki were free and fighting alongside the Magic Sword instead of against it.

"This must be Dinki's doing!" grinned Rinki, delightedly.

"About time too," grumbled Stinki, still wishing he'd been given the Slippers of Invisibility.

Elsewhere Gung-Ho had gathered his wits at last and was advancing towards the Kung-Fu Pigs. Magic Sword or no Magic Sword, he was still an opponent to be feared.

Dinki saw what was happening.

"Magic Sword! Defeat Gung-Ho!"

The sword turned and sped towards its former master.

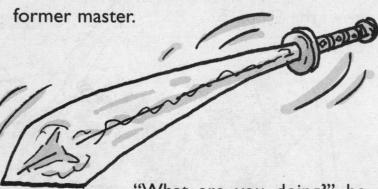

"What are you doing?" he squealed. "You're supposed to obey me, you treacherous lump of molten metal!"

Gung-Ho raised his fighting staff, only to see it chopped into pieces, like a sausage at one of the emperor's banquets.

"Leave me alone!" he howled. With his staff reduced to a useless stump, the rebel general knew he was beaten. He sank to his knees and begged for mercy.

Dinki took off her slippers and stood before the rebel leader. The sight of this pretty young pig appearing out of thin air was too much for the rest of Gung-Ho's army. They turned tail and fled.

Gung-Ho himself surrendered on the spot.

The Magic Sword returned to Dinki's grasp, its work done. The threat to the emperor had passed and the Kung-Fu Pigs had saved the empire once again.

# CHAPTER 11

*"The storm has passed, but the wise farmer knows there will be more."*
Wiy-I-Man. Pong Dynasty

Anyone passing along the Tofu road that fine morning would have seen three pigs and one wolf en route to the emperor's palace. It was of course the Kung-Fu Pigs and their unhappy prisoner, the Lord Gung-Ho.

Stinki was pleading with Dinki to let him try the Magic Sword or the Slippers of Invisibility.

"Just a quick go. No one would know."

Rinki couldn't see the harm in it either. "We'd give them straight back…"

But Dinki knew better. She knew the power that magic can exert over impression-able young pigs. She had felt it herself whenever she was close to that sword.

She thought of Oinky No Ho and seemed to hear his voice, speaking calmly and wisely. Suddenly Dinki knew what she must do. "Magic sword! Throw yourself to the bottom of that lake!"

Rinki and Stinki couldn't believe their ears.

TOO LATE! The obedient sword was already flying through the air, on its way towards the deep, deep waters of the Lake of the Six Storks. There, it would sink down, far beyond the reach of pig or wolf, coming to rest, eventually, on the sandy bed, out of sight, and forgotten for as long as you or I shall live…

Beyond the
shutters and
the gravelled
courtyard, pigs in
blue silk were
carrying the emperor's
possessions back
to his palace.
A magnificent
banquet was being
prepared, and
Ping-Pong had
made himself
guest of honour.

He clapped his trotters delightedly when he saw the Kung-Fu Pigs bowing low before him.

"I always knew you would save the day," he squeaked, somewhat untruthfully, before giving the order for Gung-Ho to be taken away. He would be put to work in the terrible Rice Mines of Long-Gon.

"I would offer you something to eat," continued the emperor, "but I don't have many courses to spare and besides I believe Oinky No Ho would like to speak with you in his garden."

Stinki gazed hungrily at the mountains of food which were arriving by the minute. "Do we have to?" he grumbled under his breath.

"Yes, we do," answered Rinki. And then they turned as one to the emperor and made a low, sweeping bow.

On their way out, Stinki's stomach was still rumbling.

Back in the garden, Oinky No Ho nodded contentedly to himself when he learned of Dinki's actions. Rinki and Stinki had expected him to be angry with their friend but not a bit of it.

"You have understood much, learned Dinki. Now give me back the magic slippers and return once more, my Kung-Fu Pigs, to your daily routine..."

The Kung-Fu Pigs bowed low.
They knew that Oinky No Ho was pleased
with them and that was enough. He wasn't
one for back-slapping or high fives.

Meanwhile, in the caves below the Lo-Fat Hills, the Crimson Trotter sat sulking beneath a flickering candle. Sulking, but not defeated.

"The emperor's kingdom will be mine one day," he told himself. "And then those meddling Kung-Fu Pigs will feel my wrath!"

And he closed his eyes and started to think up a new and even more terrible plan…

# EPILOGUE

And so, once more the Kung-Fu Pigs had saved their emperor from danger. If you would like to know more about their adventures then come and see me another time, for now the bell is tolling, summoning me to prayer.

Depart in peace, and live long, honourable stranger.

### THE END

To be continued...

# Teach yourself TANGERIN

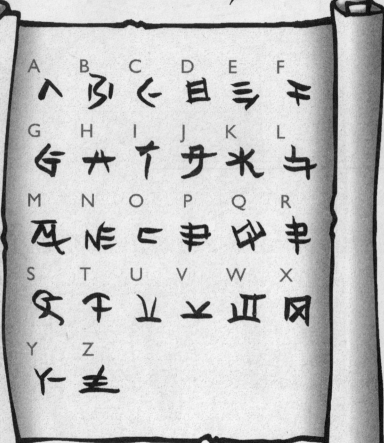

# Practice sheet

# Practice sheet